Star
Fishing

Sang-Keun Kim

Abrams Books for Young Readers

New York

It's the kind of night when
you just can't fall asleep.
You feel as though everyone
in the world is asleep but you.

"Oh, I see a light!

Is somebody awake?"

Then something marvelous happens.

Hello, Little Rabbit!

You and Little Rabbit don't speak the same language,
but somehow, you understand each other.

"You're not sleepy, either?"

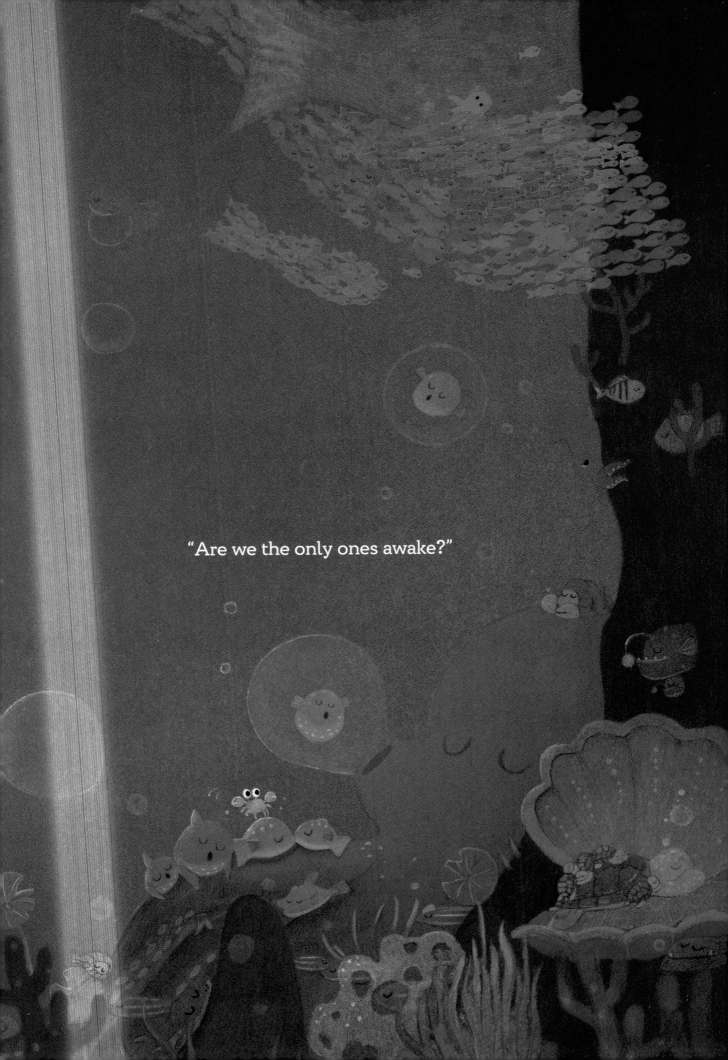

"Are we the only ones awake?"

"Crab isn't sleepy, either!"

"Are we the only ones awake?"

"Fox isn't sleepy, either!"

"Are we the only ones awake?"

"Big Bear! And Little Bear, too!"

"Why aren't any of you asleep?"

"I can't fall asleep when I'm alone."

"I'm scared to sleep alone, too!"

"I want to play, but everyone else is sleeping!"

"Me, too! That's why I'm so excited to meet you all."

Then the strings begin to move.

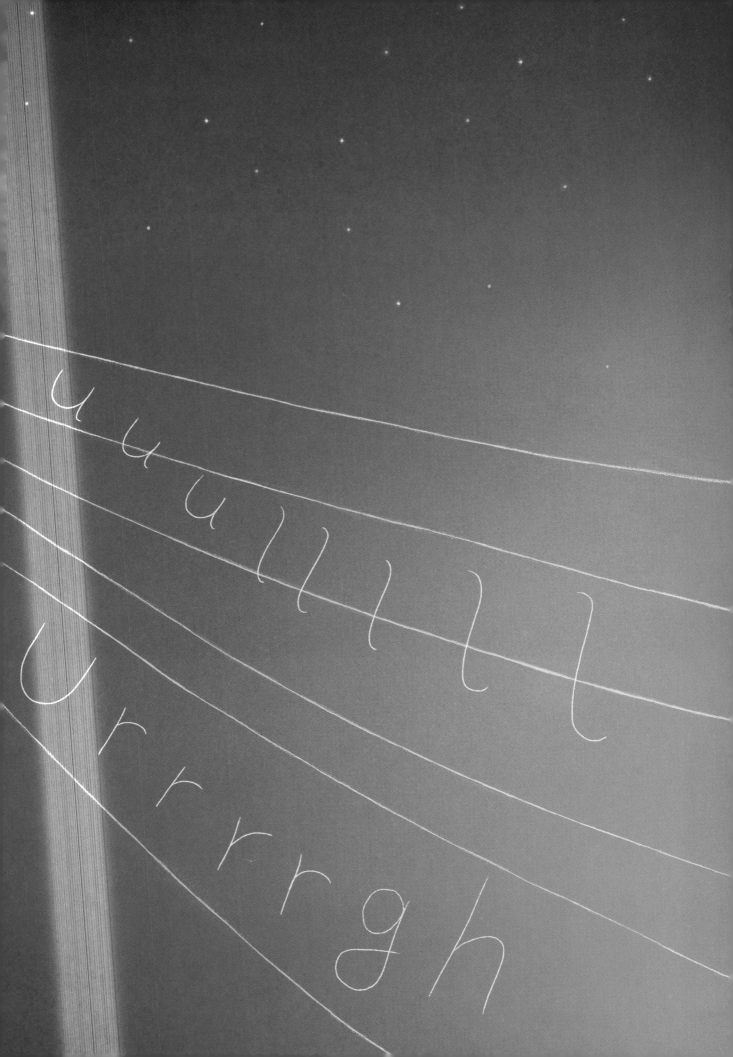

"The stars aren't sleepy, either!"

"It's so much fun to stay up late and play!"

"I wish we could come here every night."

"Little Rabbit,

when we leave,

will you be alone again?"

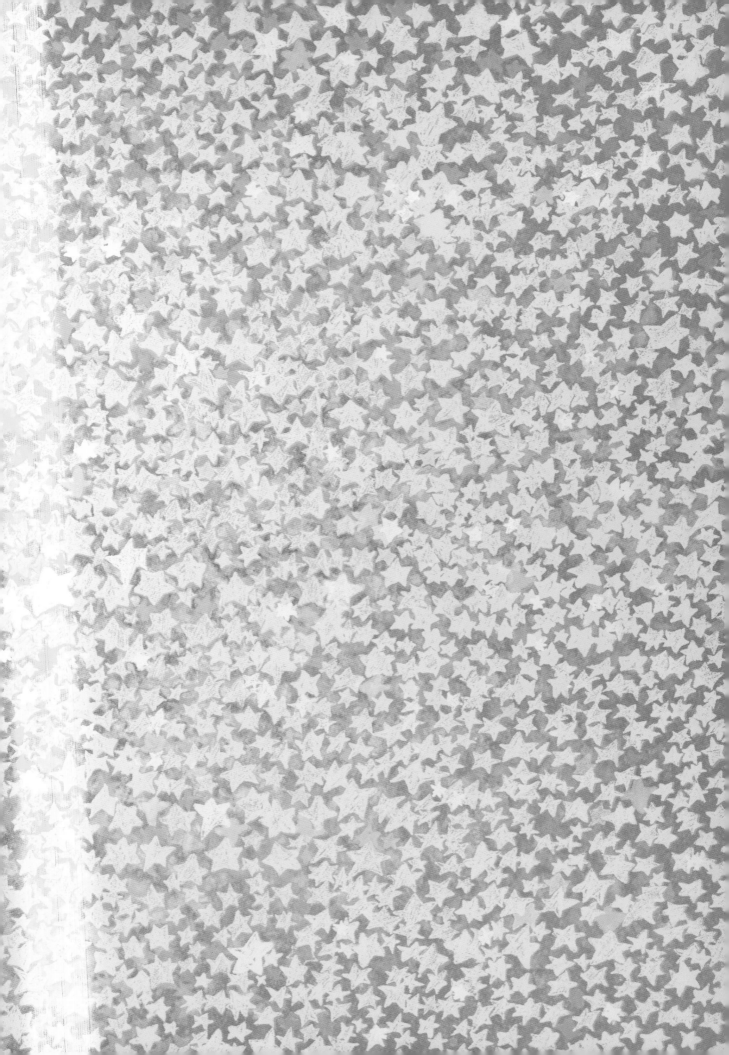

"Close your eyes for a moment, Little Rabbit."
You make constellations that will stay with Little Rabbit.

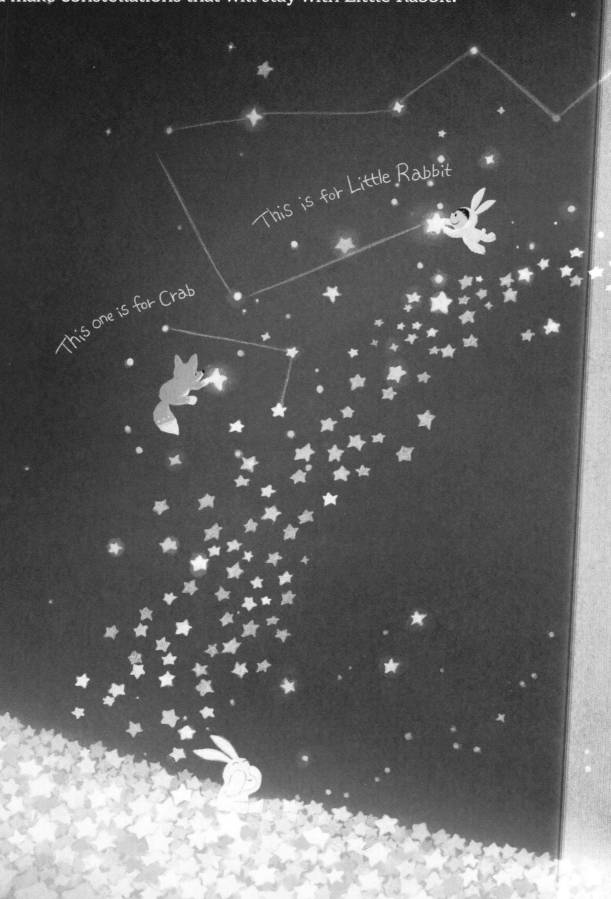

This is for Little Rabbit

This one is for Crab

This is for Fox

And this is for Big Bear
and Little Bear

But your eyelids are
starting to feel heavy.

Little Rabbit cuddles you,
one by one,
until you drift off to sleep.

Pat pat pat pat

"But I'm not sleepy..."

Little Rabbit sends their new friends home,
careful not to wake anyone . . .

...and curls up tight under the stars.

It's the kind of night
when everyone is fast asleep.

Goodnight,
dear Little Rabbit.

For my Little Rabbit, who has always watched over me.

*It was my wish to capture the warmth between those who connect
with one another effortlessly. I hope that on a sleepless night,
all the lonely hearts in the world meet, play, and find that
warm sense of connection . . . and fall into deep, sweet dreams.*

The illustrations for this book were made with colored pencil, pastel, pen, and digitally.

Cataloging-in-Publication Data has been applied for and
may be obtained from the Library of Congress.

ISBN 978-1-4197-5100-4

First published in South Korea in 2019 by Sakyejul Publishing Ltd.
Text and illustrations © 2022 Sang-Keun Kim
Translation by Ginger Ly
Book design by Heather Kelly

Printed and bound in China
10 9 8 7 6 5 4 3 2 1

Abrams Books for Young Readers are available at special discounts when purchased
in quantity for premiums and promotions as well as fundraising or educational use.
Special editions can also be created to specification. For details,
contact specialsales@abramsbooks.com or the address below.

Abrams® is a registered trademark of Harry N. Abrams, Inc.

ABRAMS The Art of Books
195 Broadway, New York, NY 10007
abramsbooks.com